Table of Contents

Where Does It Come From? 3
Photo Glossary 15
Index 16
About the Author 16

Rourke

Can you find these words?

clay

cotton

salt

windmill

Where Does It Come From?

Wood comes from trees.
People use wood to make toys.

Cotton comes from plants.

Some clothes are made from cotton.

We get **salt** from the sea.

salt

Clay comes from the ground.

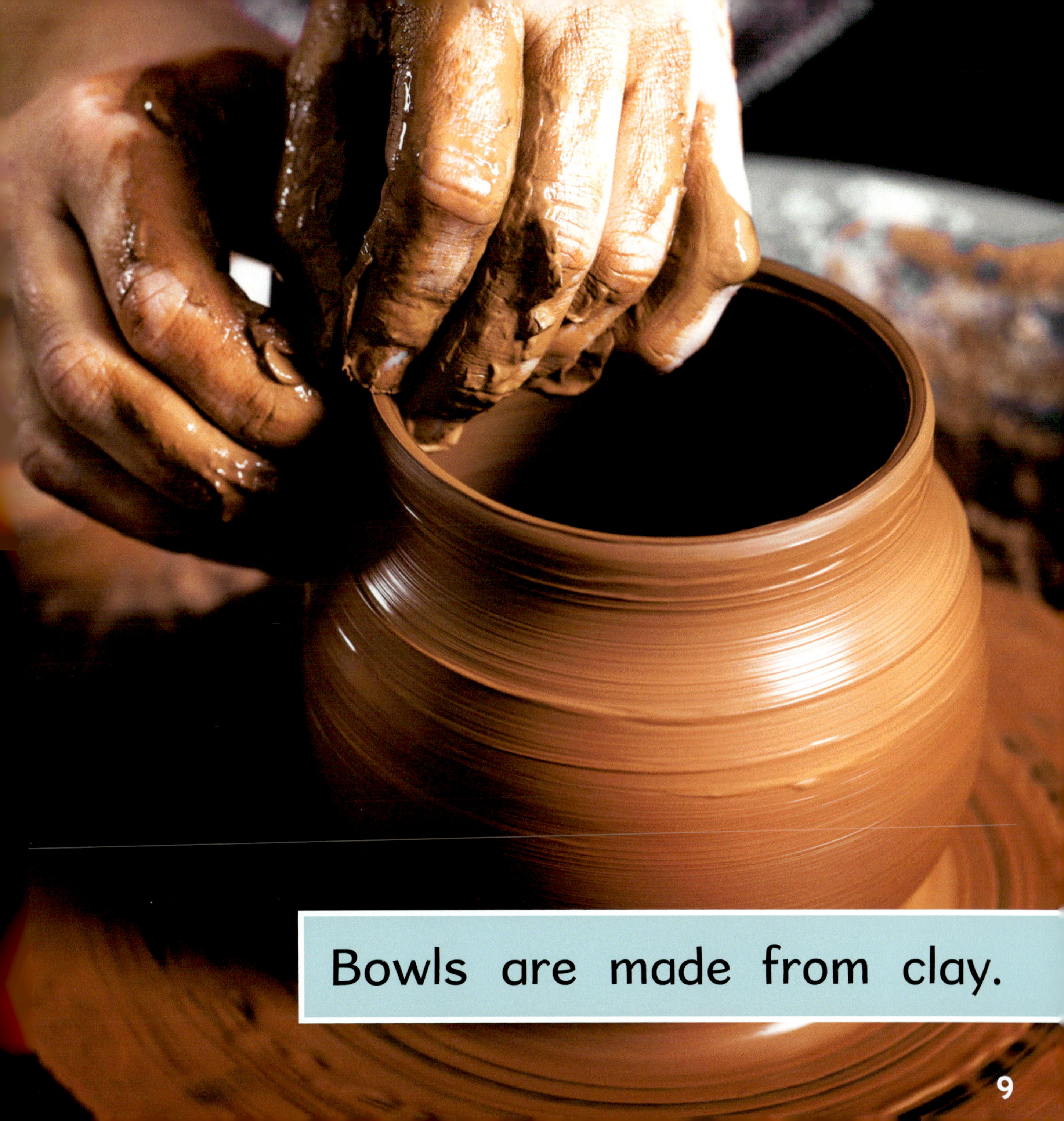

Bowls are made from clay.

Oil comes from under the ground.

Gasoline is made from oil.

A **windmill** turns wind into power.

Wind power can make our lights turn on!

Did you find these words?

Clay comes from the ground.

Cotton comes from plants.

We get **salt** from the sea.

A **windmill** turns wind into power.

Photo Glossary

clay (klay): A kind of earth that can be shaped when wet and baked to make bricks or pottery.

cotton (KOT-uhn): A plant that produces seed pods with fluffy white fibers.

salt (sawlt): A common white substance found in seawater and under the ground. Salt is used to season and preserve food.

windmill (WIND-mill): A structure with long blades that turn in the wind to produce power.

Index

clothes 5
ground 8, 10
oil 10, 11
sea 6
toys 3
wind 12, 13

About the Author

Lisa K. Schnell writes books for children. She also likes to dance, make art, and play with clay.

www.rourkebooks.com

PHOTO CREDITS: Cover: ©EvgeniiAnd; p. 2,8,14,15: ©Elena Arkadova; p. 2,4,14,15: ©Gargonia; p. 2,6,14,15: ©By voy ager; p. 2,12,14,15: ©Leigh Trail; p. 3: ©AVTG; p. 5: ©khvost; p. 9: ©YakubovAlim; p. 10: ©Sergei Dubrovskii; p. 11: ©andresr.

Edited by: Keli Sipperley
Cover design by: Kathy Walsh
Interior design by: Rhea Magaro-Wallace

Library of Congress PCN Data
Where Does It Come From? / Lisa K. Schnell
(I Wonder)
ISBN (hard cover)(alk. paper) 978-1-64156-188-4
ISBN (soft cover) 978-1-64156-244-7
ISBN (e-Book) 978-1-64156-295-9
Library of Congress Control Number: 2017957797

Printed in the United States of America
01-2902211937